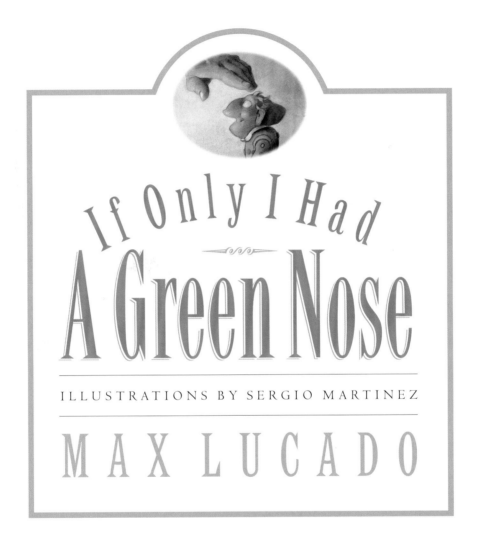

If Only I Had

A Green Nose

ILLUSTRATIONS BY SERGIO MARTINEZ

MAX LUCADO

CROSSWAY BOOKS · WHEATON, ILLINOIS

If Only I Had a Green Nose

Text copyright © 2002 by Max Lucado

Illustrations © 2002 by Sergio Martinez

Published by Crossway Books

        a publishing ministry of Good News Publishers

        1300 Crescent Street

        Wheaton, Illinois 60187

Design by The DesignWorks Group www.thedesignworksgroup.com

First printing 2002

Printed in the United States of America

LIBRARY OF CONGRESS CATALOGING-IN-PUBLICATION DATA

Lucado, Max.
If only I had a green nose / Max Lucado; illustrations by Sergio Martinez.
p. cm.
Summary: Punchinello learns that it can be difficult, foolish, and even dangerous to try to keep up with the latest fads and that Eli, his maker, gave each Wemmick different characteristics on purpose.
ISBN 13: 978-1-58134-397-7 (hc : alk. paper)
ISBN 10: 1-58134-397-3
[1. Self-acceptance--Fiction.   2. Fads--Fiction.   3. Conduct of life--Fiction.]
I. Martinez, Sergio, 1937-ill. II. Title.
PZ7.L9684   If 2002
[Fic]--dc21   2001007745

LB   16   15   14   13   12   11   10   09   08

18 17 16 15 14 13 12 11 10 9 8 7 6

To Lawson Blake

Welcome to the world!

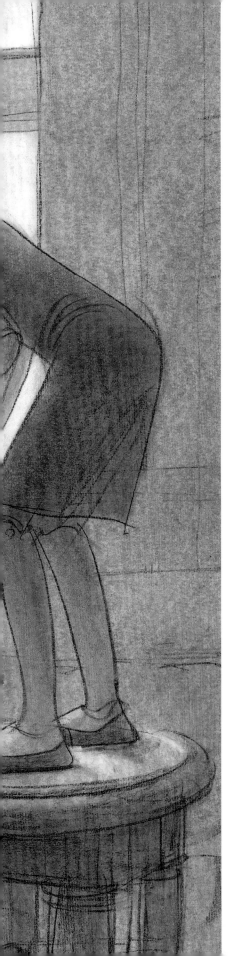

LUCIA AND PUNCHINELLO looked out the window of Eli's workshop. Like other Wemmicks, they were wooden people. But unlike the other Wemmicks, they weren't standing in line in the village below.

"Look at them all!" Punchinello exclaimed.

"I don't understand it," Lucia wondered. "Why would anyone want to paint his nose green?"

"Because everyone else is," Eli responded without looking up from his workbench.

Punchinello didn't understand. "What do you mean?"

"Everyone wants to look like everyone else. Sometimes it's square hats. Sometimes it's tall shoes. Why, last year the big thing was yellow ears. Now it's green noses. Everyone wants a green nose."

"Does a green nose make them smarter?" Punchinello asked.

"No."

"Does a green nose make them stronger?"

"No."

"Does it make them faster?"

"No."

"Then what does a green nose make them?"

Eli looked up and smiled. "Greener."

But his smile left as he looked out the window at the long line of Wemmicks. "They think they'll be happier if they look like everyone else. But I made them different on purpose. Freckles, long noses, bright eyes, dark eyes . . . these were my ideas. Now they all want to look the same."

"Not me," said Lucia. "I'm happy just the way you made me."

"Me too," agreed Punchinello. "I don't need a green nose to feel special." Then he paused and looked at the village. "But I would like to see how a green nose looks up close. Want to go?"

Eli smiled as the two stood to leave.

"Just remember, I made you different on purpose," he told them.

From street level the line looked even longer and the noses even greener. Lucia and Punchinello worked their way to the front of the crowd and watched as one Wemmick after another stepped into the nose-coloring store and came out painted.

"It's the latest thing," barked a Wemmick on the sidewalk. "Don't be the only Wemmick with a plain nose."

"Who is that?" asked Punchinello.

Lucia shrugged. "I don't know."

"Why, that's Mr. Willy Withit," volunteered a Wemmick from behind them.

"Does he run the nose-painting store?" asked Punchinello.

"More than that," the Wemmick explained. "Painted noses were his idea. So were the square hats and the tall shoes and the yellow ears. New things are his thing. He decides what is 'withit.' Isn't he the best?"

Lucia and Punchinello took a good look at this tall Wemmick with the deep voice, big smile, tall hat, and green bow tie that matched his oh-so-great green nose. Both were thinking the same question. Lucia asked it. "Who made him the new-thing picker?"

The Wemmick looked puzzled, like he'd never been asked that question. "Well, I don't know. He always has." Then his eyes brightened. "Wait, look, here comes a new nose!"

"Oooh," said the Wemmicks.

"Ahhh," admired some of the others.

The just-painted Wemmick didn't stop to speak—he just kept his nose in the air and walked past. All the green-nosed Wemmicks did this. After all, how could your nose be seen if it wasn't in the air?

Walking around high-nosed, however, was risky. Wemmicks walked into walls, doors, even each other. Lucia and Punchinello had to be very careful. One Wemmick took up the whole street.

"Step back, step back," he announced. It was the mayor. "Make way, every Wemmick. My wife is coming in for a touch-up." With one hand he waved back the citizens. With the other he guided her through the crowd.

"Horrible, just horrible," she cried, covering her nose with both hands. "I chipped some paint when I bumped into a tree. Now the real me is showing. Horrible, just horrible."

As the crowd passed, Lucia shook her head. "Such a fuss over a green nose."

"Yeah," agreed Punchinello. "You'll never catch me in the nose-coloring store."

"Aw, Punch, I was hoping you'd go."

Punchinello recognized the voice immediately. "Twiggy?" He turned and looked at the wide-eyed, sweet-smiling Wemmick. His ears began to turn red. They always did when he saw her. He reached up and covered them.

"Why don't you paint your nose, Punch? I painted mine. Everyone else is painting theirs. Besides, you'd look good in green." Twiggy reached up and touched the tip of his nose. "Yours is so cute." With that she turned and walked away. "Bye-bye." She waved.

Punchinello moved one hand from his ear to his nose. He turned and looked at his reflection in a store window.

Lucia had to grab his hand to get his attention. "Come on, Punchinello. Let's go."

As he walked past the store, he noticed Willy Withit examining his nose in a handheld mirror. Later at home, he did the same. "I never noticed before, but my nose sure looks pale."

The next morning, Punchinello walked down the street with his friends Splint and Woody.

"Are you really thinking about it?" Woody asked.

"Sort of," Punchinello answered.

"They say the paint stings your nose," Woody volunteered.

"And it stinks," Splint added.

"The brush could get in your eyes," Woody continued.

"And it only comes off with sandpaper." Splint nodded.

"Shhh." Punchinello put a finger to his lips and pointed at a large crowd of green-nosed Wemmicks standing in the square. "Something's going on."

The mayor was standing on a platform. His wife (nose freshly painted) and Willy Withit were on either side of him. "Welcome, one and all, to the first meeting of the Nosey Wemmicks Club," he announced. "Your glistening green sets you apart as a 'Withit Wemmick'." As if on cue, Wemmicks began stroking their noses. "You are classy. You are keen. You are awesome. You are green!"

Proud of his poetry, the mayor smiled, and the Wemmicks applauded. "We owe it all to Willy Withit," he shouted over the noise, "the pioneer of the painted snout!" Everyone applauded even louder.

"People love me because of you!" one shouted.

"I have more friends!" cried another.

"With a green nose, I am a better Wemmick!" exclaimed a third.

The mayor hung a medal around the neck of Willy Withit. "You have changed the face of Wemmicksville. We salute your brilliance. Without you we'd all look like . . ." The mayor paused, looking for the right word. Then he saw Punchinello and his friends. Pointing in their direction, he declared with a scornful laugh, ". . . them!"

Everyone else laughed too. Punchinello and his two friends lowered their heads and covered their noses.

"Let's hear it for Willy Withit," shouted the mayor, "the Wemmick who discovered the cure for the common nose!"

As the townspeople shouted and applauded, Woody, Splint, and Punchinello quickly turned and walked away. They didn't stop until they stood in front of the nose-coloring shop. Within a matter of minutes all three were painted and walking down Wemmick Lane.

"Hey, Punchinello," asked Splint, pushing his nose upward, "am I doing it right?"

Punchinello didn't look, "I can't see you, Splint. If I turn, my nose won't be in the air."

"Whew, this is tough work," Woody added. "Not only do you have to get painted, but you have to walk weird."

"Yeah, but doesn't it feel great to be withit?" Punchinello asked.

And for a few days it did. They hung out with other green-noses and made weekly visits to the nose-a-curist for a nose-polish. They bought nose-gloves for cold days and nose-brellas for rainy ones. All three read Willy Withit's new book, *Winner by a Nose*. Most of all, they enjoyed looking down their noses at the unpainted Wemmicks.

One day when they were feeling especially smug, Splint said to Punchinello, "I just can't imagine who wouldn't have a green nose."

Punchinello agreed, "Anyone without a green nose is so . . ."

"So what?" a voice interrupted. It was Lucia.

Punchinello was embarrassed. "I haven't seen you in a while," he said.

"You haven't seen anyone in a long time," she replied, "except yourself."

He started to speak, but didn't. He was bothered by what she said.

And he was even more bothered by what he saw. He saw it the next morning as the three were walking into Wemmicksville. Standing on the other side of the road was a Wemmick with a red nose.

"He needs to get with it," they said to each other.

But then they saw another Wemmick, also with a red nose. Then a third and a fourth. By the time they were in the village, they were surrounded by red-nosed Wemmicks. And those whose noses weren't red were in line to have them painted.

"Step right up," shouted Willy Withit from the steps of his store. "Green noses are out, and red noses are in!"

"But we just got our noses painted green!" they told him.

"No problem," he replied. "Our red will cover the green. Step right up and get in style."

The three friends looked at each other sadly. "We thought we were in style," Woody moaned. What could they do but stand in line and have their noses painted red? For a few days they fitted in, until one morning they saw a blue-nosed Wemmick.

"Oh, no," they said to each other, "not again." So they changed colors.

But it was only a short time until blue noses were out, and pink noses were in.

Then pink was out, and yellow was in.

Then yellow was out, and orange was in.

Soon Punchinello and his buddies had so many layers of paint on their noses that they couldn't remember what they really looked like.

"This has to be the final color," they said the day they walked out with orange noses.

But once again they were wrong. "I'm so tired of this," Woody moaned when he saw a purple-painted Wemmick. "I wish my nose was common again."

The three sat on a rock and hung their heads. "Me, too," agreed Punchinello. "I should have listened to Eli."

"You think he would help us?"

"Why don't you ask him?"

All three turned at the sound of the familiar voice. "Lucia," they said.

"He asks about you every day," she told them.

"Is he mad?" Punchinello wondered.

"Sad, but not mad."

Punchinello looked up toward Eli's house on the hill.

"He told me to tell you to come." Lucia spoke again.

"Could I take my friends?"

"Of course."

"Would you go with me?"

"Certainly."

And so the four began the long walk up the hill to Eli's house. When they reached the top of the hill, Eli stepped out of the workshop and began walking toward them. He met them in the yard. One by one he examined their noses.

"Been trying to fit in, eh?"

Punchinello nodded.

"Did you succeed?"

"Not really. Every time we got close, someone changed the rules."

"That's the way it is."

"And my neck hurt from sticking my nose in the air," Woody added.

"You weren't built to walk that way."

"We just want to be ourselves again," Splint said.

"I'm glad to hear that."

"Can we?" they asked.

"Of course you can," Eli replied. "I'll always help you be who I made you to be." Then he reached in his pocket and pulled out a piece of sandpaper. "But it's going to take some time."

And so Punchinello and his friends followed their maker into his workshop where he spent the rest of the day removing the paint. It hurt to be sanded, but it was worth it to be normal again.